TO THE WONDERFUL
DELANEYS,
with love from the silliest silly in the land.

AUTHOR'S NOTE: The inspiration for this retelling of "The Three Sillies" was
Joseph Jacobs's 1890 classic, *English Fairy Tales*. In his notes and references he
gives credit to an earlier version from the journal *Folk Lore* that "was communicated
by Miss C. Burne." He also mentions one that was "told in Essex at the beginning
of the century," and another from the collection of the Brothers Grimm.

First U.S. edition 1999

Library of Congress Cataloging-in-Publication Data
Kellogg, Steven.
The three sillies / Steven Kellogg. — 1st ed.
p. cm.
A retelling of The three sillies by Joseph Jacobs
Summary: A young man believes his sweetheart and her family are the three silliest
people in the world until he meets three others who are even sillier.
ISBN 0-7636-0811-4
[1. Folklore — England.] I. Jacobs, Joseph, 1854-1916. Three sillies. II. Title
PZ8.1.K3Tj 1999
398.2'0942'02 — dc21
[E] 98-30646

2 4 6 8 10 9 7 5 3 1

Printed in Hong Kong

This book was typeset in Tempus Sans ITC and Gararond.
The illustrations were done in ink and watercolor.

Candlewick Press
2067 Massachusetts Avenue
Cambridge, Massachusetts 02140

THE THREE SILLIES

Steven Kellogg

CANDLEWICK PRESS
CAMBRIDGE, MASSACHUSETTS

Once upon a time

there was a farmer and his wife who had one daughter, and she was courted by a gentleman.

Every evening he stopped to supper, and the daughter was sent to the cellar to draw the cider.

One night, just as the daughter turned on the tap, she noticed a mallet in the beams, and she began a-thinking.

Suppose him and me was to be married.

And we was to have a teeny tiny son.

And he was to grow up to be a fine young man.

And suppose our son was to come down into the cellar to draw the cider..

And the mallet was to fall on his head.

What a dreadful thing it would be.

HERE LIES OUR SON, DONKED BY A MALLET

And she began a-crying.

Well, the girl failed to return with the cider, and finally her mother went down to see what was a-keeping her.

"Look at that horrid mallet!" shrieked the daughter, and she confessed all that she had been a-thinking.

| Married. | A teeny tiny son. | All growed up. | Drawing the cider. | DONKED! | Dead. |

"Dear, dear!" said the mother, and she began a-crying too.

Then after a while the father went down to look for them.

"Look at that horrid mallet," screamed the mother, and she told him all that their daughter had been a-thinking.

| Married. | A teeny tiny son. | All growed up. | Drawing the cider. | DONKED! | Dead. |

"Dear, dear, dear!" said the father, and he started a-crying.

At last the gentleman got tired of waiting, and he went to draw a sip of cider for himself. And wasn't he surprised to find the farmer and his wife and daughter a-sobbing and a-screeching and a-swimming in the cellar full of cider.

The gentleman burst out a-laughing.

"In all my travels I've never met three sillier sillies," said he.

"Now I shall set out traveling again, and when I can find three sillies who are even sillier than you three, I'll come back and marry your daughter."

And the gentleman left them all a-wailing worse than before!

After traveling awhile the gentleman came upon an old woman who was teaching a cow to spring onto the roof of her cottage to eat the weeds that were a-growing there.

The old woman insisted.

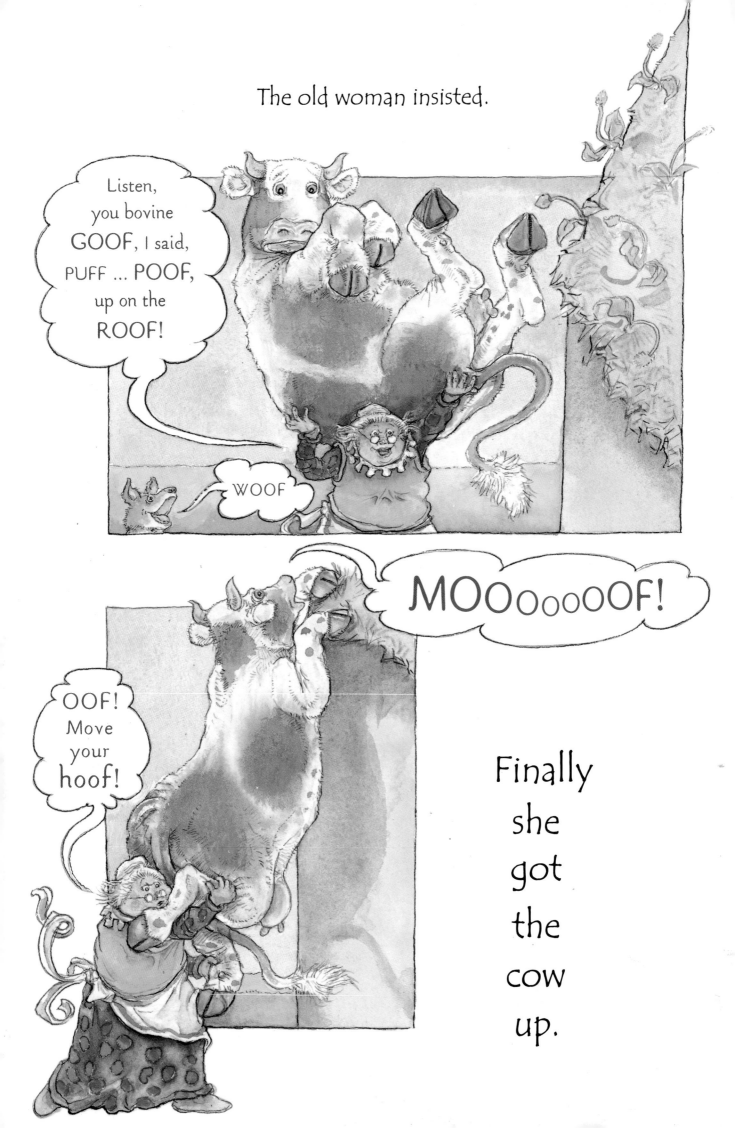

Finally she got the cow up.

Then the old woman fastened a string around the cow's neck, and passed it down the chimney, and tied the other end to her wrist.

"Quite daft!" said the gentleman, and he took his leave.

The gentleman hadn't gone far when he was overtaken
by a funeral procession, and he heard a dreadful tale.
It seemed the old woman's cow had tumbled off
the roof, and the weight of the cow had pulled
the old woman into the chimney, and she
got stuck halfway up and was
smothered in soot.

A-TUMBLED

A-YANKED

A-SMOTHERED

Well, that was the FIRST big silly.

The gentleman traveled on and on and on and on and

on until he came to an inn at dusk. The inn was so full that the innkeeper put him in a double-bedded room.

Here's the room you'll have to share with Neddie and his teddy bear.

In the morning the gentleman was surprised to see his roommate hang his trousers on the knobs of the chest of drawers and try to jump into them.

He tried over   and over   and over again.

But he couldn't manage it.

"Look, try it this way," said the gentleman, and he showed the fellow how to put his trousers on.

The fellow
proceeded
to pop
his trousers
on and off
and up and down
until he had
quite
mastered
the skill.

Then he burst joyfully into song!

The gentleman's travels soon brought him to a village,
and outside the village there was a pond, and around the
pond was a crowd of people with rakes and brooms
and pitchforks, a-whining, a-whimpering,
and a-wailing.

The gentleman asked what was the matter.
"Why," they said, "matter enough! The moon's
tumbled into the pond, and we can't get her out."
The gentleman burst out laughing.
"Look up into the sky. It's only the moon's
reflection!" he exclaimed.

Well, that was DOZENS of SILLIES!

But before the gentleman could
complete his list, the crowd became
a-restive, a-riled,
and a-riotous.

SCOUNDREL!

CHURL!

VARMINT!

IDIOT!

DOLT!

And so he took his leave.

The gentleman was heartened by the joyous welcome that awaited him.

"Dear, sweet, simple-minded sillies," he said. "In my travels I have met dozens of sillies who are far sillier than yourselves. Therefore I shall keep my promise. Let us be married at once!"

They hastened to the chapel.

After the wedding all of the guests
were invited to celebrate at the farmhouse.

The gentleman went to the cellar to draw jugs
of cider so that all could toast his new bride.

Just as he turned on the tap, the galumphing footsteps of the dancers above joggled the mallet loose.

Down it fell, directly DONKING the gentleman.

Then it bounced back and settled itself on the very beam from which it had been dislodged.

Stunned, the gentleman keeled over and rolled under the flowing tap.

The entire keg of cider had drained into the gentleman before he was discovered by his bride. She hauled him back to the celebration.

It wasn't long before the gentleman and his wife were blessed with a child.

The proud parents imagined a brilliant future for their son.

Finally the tyke spoke for himself.

And so those three sillies set off around the world in search of silly adventures, and they lived forever afterward in blissful silliness.